DISTRICT ⑬

FIGHTING THE LEGEND

Andrew Bacskai

SADDLEBACK
EDUCATIONAL PUBLISHING

SADDLEBACK
EDUCATIONAL PUBLISHING
www.sdlback.com

ISBN-13: 978-1-61651-278-1
ISBN-10: 1-61651-278-4
eBook: 978-1-60291-948-8

Printed in Guangzhou, China
0910/09-52-10

16 15 14 13 12   1 2 3 4 5

1

"Red 19! Red 19! Set! Hut! Hut!"

Helmets and pads cracked together. Ty Wilson ran to the right. He took the hand-off. Nate blocked a defender. Ty ran past them.

A defender was on Ty's right. Ty stopped and spun away. Then he took off. He made it to the end zone. Touchdown! No one ever caught Ty in the open.

Ty jogged back to the huddle. His teammates slapped his back. Ty was their star running back. But he hadn't been running well lately.

"You're a beast, Nate," Ty said. He jumped up to bump chests with him. Nate was much taller than Ty.

"That was a sick move," Nate said. He smacked the top of Ty's helmet. "You bring that in Friday's game, man. We'll win the playoffs for sure. Your little brother can't hit what he can't catch."

It was Monday. East High was practicing new plays. The championship game was on Friday. They were playing West High.

Both teams had perfect records. And one of Tyrone Wilson's sons played on each team. Both of them were in eleventh grade.

Tyrone Wilson used to play for East High. He held all the rushing and scoring records. But he didn't have a good record as a father. He was just never around.

"Well done, Ty Two!" Coach Steele barked. "Just like your old man!" His voice boomed across the field. The West team could probably hear him. And they were across town.

Coach played with Ty's dad. That was the last time East won the playoffs. He often compared Ty to his father.

Ty took a long drink of water. He poured the rest over his head. "My old man," Ty said angrily. "Did you know he left another woman and kid?"

"Yeah, you told me," Nate said. He mopped sweat from his forehead. "Take it easy, man. Don't think about it. Keep your focus."

They practiced another play. At the snap, Ty broke right again. The quarterback tossed him the ball. Nate blocked the defender in front of him. Ty tripped and fell. The ball bounced away. A defender grabbed it and ran for the end zone.

"Damn!" Ty swore. He pounded his fist on the ground. It seemed he couldn't do anything right.

"No worries, Two!" Coach Steele said. "Shake it off!"

"I've had it for today!" Ty shouted.

He ripped off his helmet and stomped to the locker room.

"Hey, Two, get back here! Practice isn't over yet!" barked Coach Steele.

"No! I'm done! And drop the Two, huh, Coach?" Ty yelled. "I ain't my dad!

2

The West High team's mood was
bright. Marcus crouched on the line.
Marcus was Ty's half brother. He
was also West's middle linebacker.

Marcus was small for a
linebacker. But he was very quick.
He darted past his blocker. He
tackled the running back hard. Ray
dropped the ball. It sailed toward the
sideline.

"Bang, baby!" Kenny shouted. He helped Marcus up. "You bring that to the game Friday, man. Your brother won't know what hit him!"

Marcus turned to Ray. Smiling, he helped Ray up. "Sorry," Marcus said. "You okay?"

"Mrph," said Ray. He stood bent over. He limped to the sideline.

"The human hammer. That's you, man," Kenny said. "You think Ty heard those hits? Fool will piss himself to sleep till Friday."

"C'mon, man. Ease up," Marcus said. "Ty's a good guy. He's having a hard time lately. You know that."

"I'm still gonna enjoy beating him," Ray said. "You know you want to. Let him have the records. Let him get a college scholarship. Let's us get the win."

"True enough," Marcus said. He grinned. He and Ray bumped helmets. Then he trotted back to the huddle.

Marcus worried about Ty. He wasn't doing well in football or school. Ty had fewer touchdown runs. He had more fumbles. And his grades were down. He might be kicked off the team.

3

After school Ty went next door. He sat on the steps with his friend Damon. Damon gulped an energy drink.

"'Sup, brother? How was practice?" Damon asked. He offered Ty a fist bump. Ty saw his hand was shaking.

"Not so good, man. We miss you out there," Ty said. Damon had red in his eyes. Ty knew Damon stayed up late every night. He also drank and smoked like crazy.

Damon was East's best receiver. But he got kicked off the team in September. He was failing all his classes. Then he just stopped coming to school. Damon was usually home alone. His dad only came home to sleep. His mom was dead.

"Nah," Damon said sadly. Ty thought he saw tears in his eyes. "I'd just be there to keep the d-backs busy. The team don't throw the ball no more. Not with you breakin' your daddy's rushing records."

"Ah, not you, too, D," Ty said. "I'm tired of hearing I'm just like my dad."

"Sorry, man. I guess the truth hurts," Damon said. "Too bad he blew out his knee. Now you're gonna break all his records. Maybe on Friday. Otherwise you'll do it next season."

"Yeah, we'll see," Ty said. A white SUV stopped in front of Ty's house. Marcus and his family got out.

"Looks like Super Doctor is movin' up," Damon said.

Marcus's stepdad was a doctor. A flash of envy burned in Ty's gut. He wondered, "Why does my mom only meet bums?"

"Come eat with us?" Ty asked.

"Nah, man. I'm goin' to the park," Damon said. "That's too much West Side for me."

4

Ty and Marcus's families ate together often. Ty was a baby when Tyrone left Londa. He wanted to be with Michelle. Michelle was pregnant with Marcus.

Then Michelle found out about Londa and Ty. She kicked Tyrone out of her house.

Somehow, Londa and Michelle became best friends. And Ty and

Marcus were close too. It sounded like a crazy TV show. But they were pretty happy.

"Londa, did you make a pie?" Marcus asked. He ate his greens.

"I sure did, honey," Londa said. "I'll go warm it up."

"I'll do the dishes, Mama," said Dee Dee. Dee Dee was Ty's half sister. She was eight years old. Her daddy didn't stay around either.

Londa was a singer. A lot of men wanted to date her. The sexy singer interested them. They didn't stay after they learned she had kids.

Michelle looked at Ty. He pushed his food around his plate. "Not hungry, baby?" she asked.

Ty shrugged. "Talk to me, Ty," she said. "I hear your grades are down. You might miss Friday's game. What's going on, sweetie?"

Marcus saw that Ty was upset. He joked, "Make sure your butt's on the field. 'Cause I'm gonna knock you on it."

Ty slammed his fork down. "I hate it that people say I'm like Dad!" he yelled. "Why can't folks see what he is? He's a damn punk! He runs away from everything!"

Darrell spoke up. "A man can make bad decisions, Ty. That doesn't make him a bad man."

"What do you know, Super Doc?" Ty shouted. "Being rich don't mean you got all the answers."

Londa was shocked. "Ty! Apologize. RIGHT NOW!"

Ty stood up fast. "I'm out of here!" He stomped out. The door slammed.

5

Marcus found Ty at the park. He was at the basketball court with Damon. They were shooting hoops.

Damon spotted Marcus first. "Check it out! West Side Boy walking these mean streets."

"'Sup, Damon," Marcus said.

"Just livin' the dream," Damon said. He was watching three boys behind Marcus. They were about fourteen years old. They sat on a bench beside the court. Damon dropped the ball. It bounced toward Marcus. Damon walked over to the boys.

Marcus grabbed the ball. "Look alive!" he called. He passed the ball. Ty squeezed it in his hands. He banged it twice on his forehead.

"I'm sorry, M. I didn't mean anything," he said softly. "You got a good thing with Darrell. That's cool."

"Yeah, it is," Marcus said. "But this ain't about me. I'm gonna tell it to you straight. What Dad does has nothing to do with us. You have to move on, Ty. Quit feeling sorry for yourself."

"Easy for you to say!" Ty said.

He zipped the ball back to Marcus. "You're on easy street now."

Marcus sighed and shook his head. He said, "There you go again, man. Crying about what everyone else has.

"Damn, Ty. Most people would kill for your talent and brains. Easy street? Let's talk easy street! You got college scouts at every game. You could get a free ride.

"You know I'm not good enough. Nobody's looking at me. And I have to work hard to get Bs. You used to ace nearly every class. You could again without hardly trying."

Ty stood quietly. He folded his arms across his chest. He looked down at his Jordans. Marcus knew he was getting through to him.

"Yeah, what I got is good," Marcus added. "But you've got a good life too, Ty. Don't screw it up."

Marcus squared up and shot the ball. It banged hard off the rim. It landed by Damon and the boys. Damon took some bills from one of them. He slapped a small bag in the boy's hand.

Damon picked up the ball. He walked back to Ty and Marcus. He was smiling. "What the hell was that?" Marcus asked.

"C'mon, now," he replied. "Man's got to earn."

"Earn what? A prison cell?" Marcus said.

Damon threw his head back and laughed. "Dang! You been on the West Side too long, brother."

Marcus looked Ty in the eye. "Only two of us here are brothers," Marcus said. He walked back to the house.

6

Ty sat on the bench Tuesday after practice. Everyone else had gone inside. Ty's elbows were on his knees. His face was in his hands.

He thought about what happened during practice. He fumbled the ball once. He dropped a screen pass. He ran the wrong way on two running plays. This sure didn't feel like easy street.

Ty felt the bench crack and groan. A huge hand dropped on his shoulder. It was Nate.

"Forget about it, Ty," he said. "Nothing matters till Friday. You've been carrying our sorry asses for two years. It's our turn to carry you, man. We got your back."

He stood and offered Ty his hand. "Let's go," he said. "Time to hit the showers."

Coach Steele was waiting. "Great work today, Nate," he said. "Ty, let's talk out here a bit."

Ty was too ashamed to look at Coach. "You're benching me, right? I understand," he said. "I sucked today. And I shouldn't have run off yesterday. I'm sorry about that."

"You kidding me, Ty? I've been

coaching for fifteen years. Benching you would be the worst move ever. This team needs you, son. You're the best damn player I've ever seen. And you know I've seen a lot of great players."

"Yeah," Ty sighed. "I know. Like my dad."

"Yes, like your dad. But you're also your own man. I shouldn't keep comparing you to Tyrone.

"I'm just afraid you're going to bench yourself, Ty. Your grades are dropping."

Ty snorted. "Guess I ain't like my old man after all."

Coach shook his head. "Who are you trying to punish? Your dad or yourself? Listen to me, son. Like it or not, you got his smarts and talent.

Maybe more than he had. And it makes me sick to watch so much talent wasted.

"You're mad at your dad? Good! Use your anger. Break his records! Win two championships instead of one! Go to college and get an education! Go pro! Do everything he didn't do, Ty. Folks will forget all about your old man."

Tears were running down Ty's cheeks. Coach lowered his voice. He put a hand on Ty's shoulder. "Here's the scoop, Ty. Ms. James told me mid-term English papers are due this week. Get at least a B and you can play Friday. Look at me, Ty. I know you can do it."

Ty looked Coach Steele in the eye. He wasn't going to let Coach or the team down. "Yeah, Coach," he said. "I can do it."

7

Five hours later, Ty wasn't so sure. Londa was working until 1 a.m. Ty was on "Dee Dee duty." She went to bed an hour ago. He'd been staring at the computer screen ever since.

Ty tried to steer his thoughts back to his paper. But he couldn't stop thinking about his younger half brother. He'd never met him. Eight years old. The same age as Dee Dee.

"Poor little guy must be hurtin' bad," Ty thought. "Does he cry himself to sleep? Is he angry? Is he fighting at school? Does he blame himself? Hard to believe one man could cause so much pain."

"Hell with him," Ty said. He pushed back from the desk. He went to look in on Dee Dee. She had fallen asleep reading. Ty put the book on her night table. He turned off her light and left the room. He walked to the front door.

Ty stepped out on the front porch. The cool air hit his face. He noticed he could see his breath. He also could feel deep bass thumping in his chest. It was Damon's stereo next door. Damon was sitting on his front steps. He had a beer in his hand.

"My pops ain't been around for a minute," Damon said. "Why don't you drag your ass over here. You look like you could use a good time."

8

Marcus was asleep at his desk. His face was on his math book. His cell phone buzzed. It woke him up. He turned and looked at the clock. It was 10:45 p.m. He answered the phone.

"Marcus?" It was Dee Dee. She was crying.

"Dee Dee? What's goin' on?" he asked.

"Marcus! I woke up and I'm all alone!" she cried.

"Calm down, Dee," he said. "Where's your mom? Where's Ty?"

"Mama's working," she said. "There's lots of people at Damon's. I think Ty's there."

"Damn," Marcus thought. He said, "Sit tight, girl. I'm coming over."

Marcus walked into the living room. Darrell was on the couch watching a game.

"What's up, Marcus?" asked Darrell.

"Dee Dee woke up alone and can't find Ty," Marcus said.

"Let's go," said Darrell.

Marcus and Darrell drove to the house. Dee Dee unlocked the door.

She ran into Marcus's arms. She rested her head on his chest.

"Marcus will stay with you, baby," Darrell said. "I'll go get your brother."

Darrell banged on Damon's door. No one answered. He let himself in. Smoke hung in the air. It stung Darrell's eyes. People lay on the floor, chairs, and couches. They seemed too tired or drunk to move. The music thumped softly. The party was out of gas.

"Check it out. Super Doc came to my party," Damon said. He got up from the couch.

"I've come for Ty," Darrell said. "Where is he?"

"Hell if I know," Damon said. "You took the fun outta him. He won't drink or smoke with a friend. You believe that?"

"Ty knows better than to follow you. You're headed down the sewer, Damon. Ty's smarter than that."

Damon got in Darrell's face. "I got a question for you, Doc," Damon growled. His breath stank of smoke and beer. "How about I bust your head open? Will you be able to patch it up?"

The door to the backyard opened. Ty came inside. "That's enough, D," he said. "Sit your ass back down."

Damon faced Ty. His mouth twisted into a nasty grin. "Go on home, little boy," he said. "This ain't your place."

Ty walked over to Darrell. "I'm sorry you had to come here," Ty said.

Darrell put a hand on Ty's shoulder. He said, "What were you thinking, Ty? Leaving Dee Dee alone in the house."

"I wasn't thinking," Ty said. "And I'm sorry. It won't happen again."

Ty looked at Damon. "You're right," he said. "This ain't my place at all.

Ty smiled at Darrell. Let's go."

9

It was Thursday afternoon. East's practice was over. The team met in the end zone.

Everyone was happy. Their star was back! Ty ran past, around, and over the defense. No one could stop him!

Coach Steele spoke softly. "This is the best team I've ever coached.

I'm proud of each of you. Winning or losing tomorrow won't change that.

"So enjoy this. You're playing a championship game! They don't come around too often. This is special, and so are you guys."

The players went into the locker room. They chanted, "Steele! Steele! Steele! Steele!"

Ty and Nate walked together. "Man, you're like a snow plow out there," Ty said.

Nate laughed. "What can I say, T," he said. "I like watching you celebrate touchdowns. You sure make an ass out of yourself."

Coach Steele caught up to Ty. He grabbed his shoulder pads. "Ms. James said you turned in your paper. You do good work?"

"I think so," Ty replied. "I guess we'll find out tomorrow."

10

City Stadium was packed. Half
the fans wore West High's purple
and gold. The other half wore the
black and red of East. Cheerleaders
jumped and twirled their batons.
The sound of marching bands filled
the air.

West had taken the field first to
warm up. Marcus stretched his legs
out in a V. His gut was buzzing with

nerves. He stared at the tunnel. The East team would be out soon.

"Is he playing?" asked Kenny. He lay down on his back. He tucked his left leg under him.

"Don't know," Marcus said. "We'll find out any time now."

A moment later, the fans roared. The East players sprinted from the tunnel.

Marcus looked for number 33. He didn't see it. He started to give up hope. Then Ty stepped out from behind number 77.

Marcus got to his feet. He went to the 50-yard line to meet Ty.

Ty gave Marcus a firm hug. "I ever tell you purple ain't a man's color?" he asked.

Marcus smiled. "Good to see you,

Ty," he said. "Game wouldn't be no fun if I couldn't pound you."

"You, too, bro," Ty said. "But you're gonna wish I hadn't made it."

"No way," Marcus said. "This is the place for you."

East won the coin toss. They chose to receive first. West's kickoff sailed high and deep. East's returner caught the ball at the 3. He ran it to the 25. The East offense and West defense took the field.

The East quarterback called the signals. "Red 19! Red 19! Set! Hut! Hut!"

Ty took the handoff. He ran behind number 77. Nate tackled the West end. "That's gonna hurt," thought Marcus. He ran around a blocker. Then he went to stop Ty.

The brothers dipped their shoulders. They prepared for contact. Crack! Both sides of town could hear the impact.